D1395883

For the two Abbies
K.W.

For my grandmother, Elsie Stockley,
from Amelia

OXFORD

UNIVERSITY PRESS

Great Clarendon Street, Oxford OX2 6DP

Oxford University Press is a department of the University of Oxford.
It furthers the University's objective of excellence in research, scholarship,
and education by publishing worldwide in

Oxford New York

Athens Auckland Bangkok Bogotá Buenos Aires
Cape Town Chennai Dar es Salaam Delhi Florence Hong Kong Istanbul
Kolkata Karachi Kuala Lumpur Madrid Melbourne Mexico City Mumbai
Nairobi Paris São Paulo Shanghai Singapore Taipei Tokyo Toronto Warsaw
and associated companies in Berlin Ibadan

Oxford is a registered trade mark of Oxford University Press
in the UK and in certain other countries

First published 2001

British Library Cataloguing in Publication Data available

ISBN 0 19 279064 1 (hardback)
ISBN 0 19 272470 3 (paperback)

Typeset by Mike Brain Graphic Design Limited

Printed in Malaysia

Granny
on the
Ark

Kathy Weston

Illustrated by Amelia Rosato

OXFORD
UNIVERSITY PRESS

God had told Noah to build an enormous Ark because a huge flood would soon cover the earth.

Noah was not very pleased. It was hard work, especially as he had to find two of every animal to take into the Ark.

Rain clouds were already gathering in the sky.

'Come on, boys!' he shouted to his sons Ham, Shem, and Japhet. 'We must hurry. We still have to get all the animals aboard.'

But just then –

'Yoo Hoo! Surprise!'
   Mrs Noah's mum and dad had arrived with their
little old dog Isaac.

Mrs Noah appeared from behind a giraffe. 'Mum! Dad!
What a lovely surprise. And Isaac too.'
  'What on earth is that?'
Granny pointed at the Ark.
'Are you starting a zoo?'
  'Well,' said Mrs Noah,
'there's going to be this flood
and – oh, you explain, Noah.'

So Noah told Granny why he had built the Ark and collected all the animals, and that she and Grandad must come too.

'Oh no,' said Granny. 'You needn't think I'm getting on that thing. I prefer to keep my feet firmly on dry land, thank you very much.'

Grandad put his arm around her shoulders. 'I think, dear, that Noah is saying there won't be any dry land left. Come on. It'll be an adventure. A bit of sea air will do us good.'

Granny looked at the sky. 'Well,' she admitted, 'it does *look* like rain.'

Noah was pleased.

But he wasn't looking forward to telling Granny that she'd be sharing with the elephants.

That night everyone and everything went into the Ark two by two. Then the rain began. And how it rained – buckets full, baths full, oceans full.

By the morning there was water
wherever they looked.

Isaac was far too busy chasing cats to notice the weather
– or that the window was open.
   'Isaac! Be careful!' shouted Granny – but too late.

Isaac had fallen overboard.
  'Oh my goodness!' cried Granny. 'Somebody *do* something!'

'Don't worry, Gran, we'll get him for you,' Ham said, laughing, as Japhet came running with the big net they'd used to catch the crocodiles. They put the drenched and shivering little dog into Granny's arms.

'Oh, poor little Isaac. I *knew* something like this would happen!' said Granny. 'We should never have come in the first place.'

'Come on, dear,' said Grandad. 'It's time we fed those elephants, though goodness knows what they eat.'

'Well, in my experience, elephants eat buns,' said Granny.

Noah smiled and wondered how many elephants she had met, but he didn't say a word.

Things settled down after that, although poor Noah felt
seasick for a lot of the time. The animals started to have
babies and the Ark was even more crowded. Of course,
some things did go wrong. Shem, who was supposed to
be in charge of the birds, was in big trouble when Granny
found that he'd put the hens right next to the foxes.

All that was left of the hens were a few feathers and some eggs. Granny took the eggs and popped them inside her petticoat, safe and warm. 'You never know,' she smiled to herself.

There were rabbits and kittens everywhere. One of the pigs had twenty-two piglets, so the goats moved in with Granny and immediately began to eat Grandad's socks.

'I'll have those – if you don't mind,' said Granny, in a voice that even a goat couldn't argue with.

After many weeks the Ark came to rest with a
bump, right on top of a mountain.
   'Listen,' said Granny. 'Can you hear anything?'
   They all listened.
   'Not a thing,' said Shem.
   'Nor me,' said Japhet.
   'Exactly!' Granny spread her arms.
'You can't hear the rain any more.
It's stopped at last.'

So Noah looked out. There was still water all around. He let one of the ravens fly free to see if it could find land. But it came back.

After another week, Noah let a dove go, but like the raven, it found no land.

Granny was very disappointed. 'If we don't reach dry land soon, I shan't be held responsible,' she said crossly, snatching back a pair of her knickers from a monkey who was wearing them as a hat.

Noah tried once more. They all watched as the dove flew away.

'Well, fingers crossed everyone,' said Granny. 'But meanwhile, there's work to be done. Just listen to those lions. Anyone would think they hadn't been fed for a week. It's upsetting Isaac.'

Early the next morning the dove returned with an olive branch in its beak.

'If there's a tree then there must be land!' cried Noah.

He and the boys opened the door of the Ark and let the sunshine in. Two by two they all stepped ashore onto the fresh new land and gazed at the beautiful rainbow.

'It's a miracle,' Granny smiled. 'All the family together and safe. A new beginning for us all. I knew all along it was the right thing to do.'
Noah winked at Mrs Noah.

Then Granny rustled her petticoats, and they all laughed with delight as they heard the cheep of newly-hatched chicks.